SV

ACS-8962

D1505947

Fox and Fluff

WRITTEN BY
Shutta Crum

ILLUSTRATED BY
John Bendall-Brunello

ALBERT WHITMAN & COMPANY
MORTON GROVE, ILLINOIS

For Jennifer, Geoff, and Deb. – S. C.

For my nephew and niece, Lewis and Poppy,
and as always, my darling wife Tiziana. – J. B-B.

Also by Shutta Crum:
Who Took My Hairy Toe?

Library of Congress Cataloging-in-Publication Data

Crum, Shutta.
Fox and Fluff / by Shutta Crum ; illustrated by John Bendall-Brunello.
p. cm.
Summary: The first sight a newly hatched chick sees is a fox who he
thinks is his father, but a fox can't parent a chicken, can he?
ISBN 0-8075-2544-8 (hardcover)
[1. Chickens – Fiction. 2. Foxes – Fiction. 3. Parent and
child – Fiction.] I. Bendall-Brunello, John, ill. II. Title.
PZ7.C888288 Fo 2002 [E] – dc21 2002001727

The design is by Scott Piehl.

For more information about Albert Whitman & Company,
visit our web site at www.albertwhitman.com.

One evening a little white egg bounced off a farm cart and cracked open. Out hatched a fluffy round chick, just as Fox was coming along the path.

Peep!

Fox thought, What's this? A snack!

Chick thought, Who's this? Papa?

Well, Fox was about to pop the chick into his mouth when the chick cheeped, "Papa!" and pecked him on the chin.

"Hey! Watch that," warned Fox.
"I'm not your papa. I'm a fox.
I eat little bits of fluff like you.
I'll just open my mouth and
you can jump in. OK?"

So Fox opened his mouth,
showed his big, bad teeth,
and waited.

Nothing happened.

The chick was sitting with his beak
open wide, too.

Peep!

"OK, Fluff, or whatever your name is," said Fox. "Today's your lucky day. I'm just gonna walk away and forget we ever met, see? Have a great life, kiddo!"

Well, he hadn't gone too many steps when he thought he'd better have a look ... just in case.

There was Fluff, right behind him!

"How many times I got to tell you? I'm a big, bad fox. I *eat* chickens. No way could I be a papa to a chick," said Fox. "Go! Go find some feathered types."

peep!

"Poor little mixed-up thing," Fox muttered as he started to walk away.

When he turned back, Fluff was still there!

Fox sighed. "OK, Fluff, listen up. It looks like I'm stuck with you for now. But I'm hungry and I'm looking for dinner. So stay back behind me, and maybe no one will notice."

They came to a hollow log and frightened a
sleeping rabbit. Well . . .

that is, until the rabbit saw
Fluff – and laughed!

tee!hee!

They came to a shallow creek and frightened
a sun-bathing lizard. Well . . .

sort of.

They came to a leafy nest and frightened
a gray mouse. Well . . .

maybe not.

Tired and hungry, Fox and Fluff lay down on a hilltop. "Listen, kiddo, I've got nothing against you, but this just isn't working out," Fox said as they munched on some grass. "I've got a reputation to uphold. I gotta be big, I gotta be bad!"

"Grrr . . . peep!" said Fluff.

Fox yawned. "Oh, like that's *really* bad."

"Pa . . . pa," Fluff softly cheeped, snuggling up
to Fox. Fox looked down at the small yellow chick
and muttered, "Yeah, right," as he fell asleep.

The next morning Fox said, "Fluff, I've made up my mind. You've got to learn how to be a chicken. Which you are, and which I'm not. You can learn how at the henhouse. What can I give you if you stay with me, huh? Zip. Zilch!"

So Fox took Fluff to the farmyard gate and said, "Now listen up in there and you can learn lots o' nice things, like how to eat corn and how to ... (sniff) ... be frightened of foxes. Stuff I can't teach ya, see? Now shoo ... go on, be good!"

Fox felt all funny inside, watching the hens coo and cluck as they led Fluff into the henhouse.

Slowly Fox turned around and slunk off into the forest.

For the next few days, he ate mostly berries and grasses. Somehow he couldn't get up the energy to chase after his dinner.

At the henhouse Fluff leaped off buckets and
bales with wings outspread and fierce grimaces.
"Grrr . . . peeeep!" Right at the younger chicks!

He stalked the hens, crouching and running, until
he had them all cornered in the chicken coop.

He taught the chicks to yip and bark. It kept the henhouse awake all night.

Fluff was not a very good chicken.

And Fox was not a very happy fox.

In fact, Fox secretly visited the farm almost every day, hoping to get a glimpse of Fluff. And one day, there he was! The angry hens had kicked him out of the henhouse!

"Fluff!" yelled Fox, hurrying to pick him up.

So Fluff went home with his papa.

He never went back to chicken school. But he studied hard and became a famous teacher . . .

...at Papa Fox's Forest School.